This Book
Purchased in the Names of

Clare Caruso
&
Juliana Valcarenghi

Book Buddies
Summer 2004

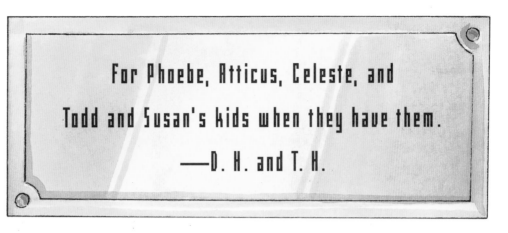

For Phoebe, Atticus, Celeste, and
Todd and Susan's kids when they have them.
—D. H. and T. H.

Text copyright © 2004 by Dennis Hebson
Illustrations copyright © 2004 by Todd Hoffman

First published in the United States of America in 2004 by Walker Publishing Company, Inc.

Published simultaneously in Canada by Fitzhenry and Whiteside, Markham, Ontario L3R 4T8

For information about permission to reproduce selections from
this book, write to Permissions, Walker & Company, 104 Fifth Avenue, New York, New York 10011

Library of Congress Cataloging-in-Publication Data
Hebson, Dennis.
Robots everywhere / Dennis Hebson ; illustrations by Todd Hoffman.
p. cm.
Summary: Various kinds of robots go about their daily activities, such as riding buses, rusting at the beach, and eating metal nuts.
ISBN 0-8027-8892-0 — ISBN 0-8027-8893-9 (rein)
[1. Robots—Fiction. 2. Stories in rhyme.] I. Hoffman, Todd, ill. II. Title.
PZ8.3.H3839Ro 2004
[E]—dc21   2003050088

The artist used Dr. Martin inks on Canson cold press watercolor paper (grain finish) to create the illustrations for this book.

Book design by Victoria Allen

Visit Walker & Company's Web site at www.walkeryoungreaders.com

Printed in Hong Kong

2 4 6 8 10 9 7 5 3 1

Robots Everywhere

Denny Hebson

Illustrations by Todd Hoffman

WALKER & COMPANY
NEW YORK

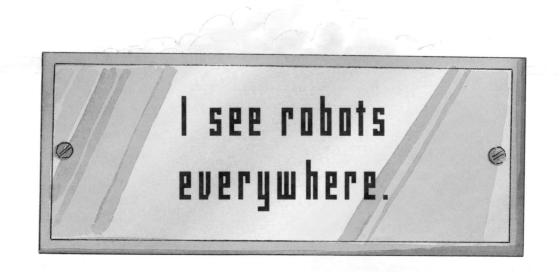

I see robots
everywhere.

Playing catch with
sewer grates.

and rusting down at Robot Beach.

Robot kids
with metal trikes.

Sleeping under sheets of foil.